Honk!
Honk!

LUCKY

THE
GOLDEN GOOSE

red truck publishing inc.
711 Fifth Ave. Suite 400 New York, NY 10022
www.redtruck.com

WRITTEN AND ILLUSTRATED BY JOHN WRENN

For Soren

Early every morn at cock-a-doodle-doo,
animals went to work on Farmer Fred's crew.
Each was responsible for their day's deeds.
Fred paid the going rate in pumpkin seeds.

The cows gave milk and cream with ease.
The goats kept the grass down below their knees.
The sheep made wool for mittens and hats.
The pigs worked on porkbellies while they sat.

The hens laid eggs in white and brown.
But the geese felt picked-on giving up down.
"Enough of this stuff!" Lucky said one day.
"I'm not just fluff and I want more pay!"

"More pumpkin seeds Fred or I walk, I say!"
Farmer Fred spat carrot juice and kept pitching hay.

"More pumpkin seeds?" poor-ol' Lucky pondered.
Then he realized,
"My seeds have been squandered!"

What if I take the seed I have today,
plant it over yonder and walk away.

After a while of growing in the ground,
it grows into a pumpkin big and round!

There would be more seeds, more seeds inside.
To plant, in turn, in more fields far and wide.
It won't be long before I'm sitting on top
of a blue chip beauty bumper pumpkin crop!

Off went Lucky to share his savings plan,
with all the animals in Farmer Fred's clan.

The pigs blinked blankly, the hens cluck clucked,
the sheep said *"Baah"*
And the ducks simply ducked.

The gaggle of geese giggled at his scheme.
   "You're a silly goose with a silly dream!"

            Gilda Goose honked in a hoity toity way,
               "I think a solid golden egg is
                        what I'd rather lay!"

Gus Goose admitted,
"*The idea sounds clever,*
but who do you think I am, J.D. Rockafeather?"

Lucky knew his idea wasn't so far astray.
If he started now,
his fortune would be great
someday!

Ignoring the honks and hisses of peers,
   he kept planting his seeds for a couple of years.
Month after month he watched his pumpkins grow.
   In no time the dividends began to show.

"Take a gander at this," Lucky said and smiled.
Pumpkins blazed golden for miles and miles.
"I guess it's not a bad idea, Gilda Goose cried,
it beats every get-rich-quick-trick I've tried!"

"I've tried them all and without any luck.
I should be sitting pretty instead of getting plucked!"
Gus Goose gulped at Lucky's great pumpkin pile,
wishing he hadn't dilly dallied all the while.

Now every day at cock-a-doodle-doo,
    the animals come to work on Lucky's work crew.
        Each has a job.
        Farmer Fred picks weeds.
    Lucky pays the going rate in pumpkin seeds!

Yes, Lucky owns the farm that once was Fred's.
But all the millions haven't gone to his head.
And all the crew is very beholden
to Lucky ol' goose whose idea proved golden!

If you take one pumpkin seed or one penny,
    saving and investing turns one in to many.